Copyright © 2003 by Michael Neugebauer Verlag,
an imprint of NordSüd Verlag AG, Gossau Zürich, Switzerland
First published in Switzerland under the title Auf Wiedersehen, Oma.
English translation copyright © 2004 by North-South Books Inc., New York

First published in the United States, Great Britain, Canada, Australia, and New Zealand
in 2004 by North-South Books, an imprint of NordSüd Verlag AG, Gossau Zürich, Switzerland.
First paperback edition published in 2005 by North-South Books. Distributed in the United States
by North-South Books Inc., New York.

Library of Congress Cataloging-in-Publication Data is available.
A CIP catalogue record for this book is available from The British Library.
ISBN-13: 978-0-7358-1894-1 / ISBN-10: 0-7358-1894-0 (trade edition) 10 9 8 7 6 5 4 3 2
ISBN-13: 978-0-7358-1895-8 / ISBN-10: 0-7358-1895-9 (library edition) 10 9 8 7 6 5 4 3 2 1
ISBN-13: 978-0-7358-2011-1 / ISBN-10: 0-7358-2011-2 (paperback) 10 9 8 7 6 5 4 3 2
Printed in Italy

Birte Müller

Felipa and the Day of the Dead

Translated by Marianne Martens

A Michael Neugebauer Book
North-South Books / New York / London

Felipa lived in a small village high up in the Andes Mountains. Her grandmother, Abuelita, had just died. She was very old. No one knew exactly how old she was. In fact, Abuelita hadn't even known herself. Felipa missed Abuelita. She had always been there, with plenty of time to talk, to listen to whatever Felipa wanted to tell her. So Felipa was very sad even though her parents told her that when people die, their souls live on forever.

But where *was* Abuelita's soul? What was she doing? Perhaps Burro, her donkey, would know the answer.

Burro just looked at her
and didn't say a thing.

Abuelita's soul had to be *somewhere*. "Come on, let's look for her," Felipa said to Chancho the pig. Pigs have very good noses. Together they searched everywhere. In the village, in the fields, and even in the cemetery. They didn't find anything. Then Felipa had another idea. Maybe Abuelita's llamas know where her soul is, she thought.

But if the llamas knew anything, they weren't telling.

Felipa was very discouraged. At bedtime she asked her mother, "Where is Abuelita's soul now? I've looked for it everywhere, but I can't find it."

"She is with the spirits, high up in the snow-covered mountains. Look how beautiful it is up there," answered her mother.

Felipa decided to go there the very next day.

Early the next morning Felipa headed off toward the highest mountain.

She walked for hours, but no matter how far she went, the mountain didn't seem to get any closer.

Felipa was hungry, and when it began to get dark, she felt a little scared.

Then she heard a voice calling, "Felipa, Feliiiippaaaa!" It was her father, coming to find her.

"I'm afraid you can't just go and visit souls," her father told her the next day. "They live in their own world. Souls live in the mountains, and in the ground, and in everything that grows. But every year in November they come to visit us and we have a big celebration for them."

Felipa waited and waited. Finally it was November. Everyone in the village was busy preparing for the celebration, cooking special treats. Felipa especially liked making little people out of sweet dough. Everything was set out on a big table and decorated with flowers and candles.

Who is going to eat all of this food? wondered Felipa. Then she realized that the souls would have come from far away and would be hungry and thirsty when they arrived.

The village celebrated with the souls for one whole day and one whole night. The streets were filled with laughter and music and wonderful things to eat. And the next morning, they brought everything up to the cemetery.

Everyone helped decorate
the graves with flowers, candles, and food.

Felipa liked the celebration at the cemetery best of all. She felt very close to Abuelita there. Felipa and her parents shared memories of Abuelita. And Felipa could talk to her again—just like she had before.

At the end of the day, Felipa felt a little sad for she knew that Abuelita couldn't stay with her. All souls had to go back to their world.
But she was hopeful, too. "Adios, Abuelita," she said softly.

"Until next year
on the Day of the Dead."

ABOUT THIS BOOK

The Day of the Dead is celebrated on November 1 throughout Latin America and in many parts of the United States. In some places, the celebrations continue on November 2. Traditions vary from place to place. Celebrations can be held in cemeteries or at home. In some places the souls of children are remembered on the first day, those of adults on the second. Ceremonies in some countries include masked dancers representing the souls themselves. But the candles, flowers, and food that welcome the returning souls are universal. And so is the spirit of remembrance—the feelings of sorrow and loss coupled with joy as people commemorate and commune with loved ones who have died.

Birte Müller first experienced the Day of the Dead when she was studying art in Mexico City. She was so fascinated by the holiday she returned several years later to witness the celebrations again. She writes, "In my native Germany we don't have anything like this, and I wanted to do a children's book that would introduce European children to this tradition. I decided to write my thesis on the Day of the Dead, and was given a scholarship to study in Bolivia. There, where the old traditions are very much alive, I participated in the celebration of 'Todos Santos' in a very small village in the Andes. Back in Germany, I spent a year writing and illustrating *Felipa and the Day of the Dead*."